ANIMAL TALES

4

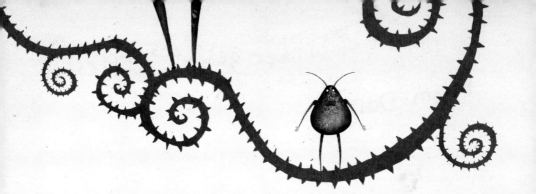

BY THE SAME AUTHOR, PUBLISHED BY PROTEA BOOK HOUSE:

Versamelde Boesmanstories 1 and 2
Dierestories 1, 2, 3 and 4
Animal Tales 1, 2 and 3

ANIMAL TALES

4

G.R. von Wielligh

Illustrated by Dale Blankenaar

Protea Book House | Pretoria | 2013

Animal Tales 4 – G.R. von Wielligh

First edition, first impression 2013 by Protea Book House
PO Box 35110, Menlo Park, 0102
1067 Burnett Street, Hatfield, Pretoria
8 Minni Street, Clydesdale, Pretoria
protea@intekom.co.za
www.proteaboekhuis.com

TRANSLATOR: Linda Michell
EDITOR: Danél Hanekom
PROOFREADER: Caren van Houwelingen
COVER DESIGN: Dale Blankenaar
BOOK DESIGN: Hanli Deysel
TYPOGRAPHY: 11.5 on 16 pt ZapfCalligr
PRINTED AND BOUND: Craft Print, Singapore

© 2013 Protea Book House (text)
© 2013 Dale Blankenaar (illustrations)
ISBN 978-1-86919-929-6

Contents

Jackal and Wolf go fishing

We discover how forgiving Wolf can be and that he learns nothing from the mishaps that befall him; no, experience leaves Wolf none the wiser!

Wolf had not crossed paths with Jackal for some time, but not for want of effort on his part. He was eager to track down his nemesis, but Jackal was equally keen to keep out of his way. Without Wolf, however, Jackal found it difficult to come by food, and so he approached Vulture to resolve the misunderstanding between himself and Wolf.

"Where's your so-called friend Jackal?" asked Wolf when he saw Vulture. "Tell me so that I can pay him back for all his sly tricks. I'm going to sort him out once and for all, that's for sure!"

"Tsk, tsk," objected Vulture. "That's no way to talk about your best pal. Don't you know how much he cares about you? The reason you two fall out all the time, old boy, is because you interfere with his plans. If you'd only listen to him and do exactly as he tells you, his clever schemes would work perfectly every time."

Wolf thought about this for a while and his pondering led him to the conclusion that he would forgive Jackal for past misdeeds after all. So off he went to make peace.

When Jackal caught sight of Wolf coming along the path, he whipped a piece of (stolen) fish out of his bag and began eating it with relish.

"Good morning, Brother Jackal!" called Wolf. "What is that tasty morsel you've got there?"

Jackal called back a friendly greeting and said: "It's some delicious fish. Would you like a piece?"

"Yes, please!" replied Wolf eagerly. "Where did you find such fine fish?"

"I caught it in the farmer's dam last night," explained Jackal with a devilish glint in his eye.

"If there are more, we should go and catch some tonight," suggested Wolf.

"I was planning to do just that," said Jackal. "The dam is crawling with fish, but we must wait until it's really late, because fish bite best after midnight."

"Right you are, Brother Jackal. I'm patient – I can wait," agreed Wolf, pleased with the prospect.

At around midnight when a biting little wind tore around the farmer's house, Jackal said: "It's time, Brother Wolf. The farmer and his dogs are asleep and the fish will be ready to bite now."

The pair set off with chattering teeth. Every now and then they stopped to shake themselves and fluff out their fur against the bitter cold.

When they reached the dam, Wolf asked: "Tell me, Brother Jackal, how do you catch fish? I've never done it before."

"Oh, there's no great art to fishing! All you have to do is lie very still at the water's edge, dangle your tail in the water, and wait for the fish to bite."

"Well, that sounds easy enough – like child's play, really," said Wolf, finding a suitable spot and lying down.

"Goodness! The water's very cold!" he exclaimed as his tail disappeared beneath the water.

Jackal checked that Wolf was in the correct position and then went to lie down a short distance away. But he did not put his own tail in the water; he kept it tucked close to his side where Wolf could not see it – nor would it occur to the dullard to come and check.

After a little while, Wolf exclaimed again: "Jeepers, Brother Jackal! The water's freezing – I think my tail has frozen solid!"

"Just keep still, Brother, you're feeling the cold fish swimming around your tail. I can feel them, too. They're getting ready to bite."

Reassured, Wolf lay still. The water began to ice over and icicles formed on Wolf's tail. "Brother Jackal, my tail is heavy with fish already!" he said. "Should I pull it out now?"

"That would be a big mistake!" replied Jackal hastily. "Only the small fish are biting now. Wait a little longer for the bigger ones."

By daybreak the dam had iced over completely. Jackal leapt up from his spot. "That's funny," he said, "I haven't caught a single fish. You have had all the luck, I can see tons of fish on your tail! Quick, pull it out! Pull as hard as you can!"

Wolf pulled and Wolf yanked, this way and that, but his tail was stuck fast. "Help me, Brother Jackal; I'll give you some of my catch if you help me."

Jackal pretended to be concerned: "If I help you pull, your tail might snap off and then you'll lose your catch and your tail. I'll tell you what – let me run home and fetch a sack, then we can take the fish off one by one."

With that Jackal ran off, but not to fetch a sack. No, he ran straight to the farmer's house where he reported that Wolf was trapped in the frozen dam. The farmer got his sjambok, whistled for his dogs and went to the dam. The whip cracked and the dogs attacked and Wolf got the beating of his life. At last he managed to free himself and fled without a backward glance.

Of Jackal and the sack there was no sign.

Baboon and Aardvark

In this story we learn about the peculiarities of Baboon and Aardvark, namely: that Baboon has no friends because of his greed and stinginess; why he is afraid of poison, gun traps and snares; why Aardvark has a thick tail, long ears and no teeth; why he eats ants and why he only comes out at night.

Baboon used to have many friends once. But he is a lazy, fun-loving chap who happily takes his pleasure at the expense of others and so he gradually lost all his friends.

Baboon was well aware of the reasons for his friendlessness. He decided to pick someone and make an effort to treat him well – and who better than patient old Aardvark who never quarrelled with anyone, not even if they robbed him blind?

Back in those days, both Baboon and Aardvark used to eat meat and plants. They often caught and killed the farmer's lambs and although he had devised all kinds of plans to stop the thieves, nothing had worked so far. Aardvark was strong and could dig himself out of any trap and Baboon was a resourceful problem-solver, especially when it came to saving his own skin.

Once, the farmer tried poisoning the pumpkins and watermelons, but Baboon knew which remedy to use to counteract the poison (he was one of Lion's doctors after all) – the poison almost killed old Aardvark, but Baboon's treatment saved him in the end.

Since then the pair exercised a bit more caution about what they ate, which is why Baboon sniffs and inspects everything carefully before he eats anything these days.

Then, the farmer tried using snares, but if Baboon got caught in one, strong old Aardvark would set him free. Baboon did not return the favour, however, and Aardvark had to rely on his own strength if he ended up in a snare.

On their daily wanderings the two friends came across an unused cage trap. They thought it was a stone shelter and sometimes they went inside to sit and chat. When the farmer became aware of this, he decided to try and capture the pair in the old trap.

Wily Baboon noticed immediately that something was amiss, however. He jumped onto the top of the stone shelter to have a look and then said Aardvark: "No, it's perfectly safe; the farmer has done some repairs; he's probably going to use it as a lamb pen. Look, there are already two lambs inside. You go in and get them while I keep watch out here."

Aardvark did as he was told, but as he crawled in, the big flat rock crashed down on his tail and blocked the entrance in the process. The painful throbbing in his swollen tail made Aardvark lose all interest in the lambs and he urged Baboon to dismantle the shelter from the outside. Baboon began rolling rocks off the top of the cage trap and when he'd made a hole that was big enough, he reached in and pulled Aardvark out by the ears – Aardvark has had long ears and a thick tail ever since.

When the farmer came to check the trap, he found he had

been outsmarted by the thieves yet again – not only had they stolen the lambs, but they'd also left the trap in ruins. The farmer gave up trying to capture the pair and put an extra effort into guarding his livestock instead – it turned out to be his best strategy yet.

One day Baboon said to Aardvark: "We haven't been able to catch a lamb in ages because the farmer keeps them in the kraal. We can't let him get away with it any longer. I've thought of a brilliant plan."

"Usually your plans end up with me being stuck and you being free, but tell me what you've got in mind," replied Aardvark.

"If we disguise ourselves with sheepskins, we can get into the kraal unnoticed along with the rest of the sheep – and once we're inside, we can catch the lambs," explained Baboon.

Aardvark agreed and they went to look for sheepskins. Along the way they came upon a small kraal where the farmer kept fruit, pumpkins and lambs from time to time. But the farmer had booby-trapped the entrance with a loaded musket.

Baboon noticed the booby trap and said to Aardvark: "Let's untie the musket and take it; it could come in very useful." Of course he ensured that Aardvark did the untying at the muzzle end, while he worked on the safer end.

As Aardvark tugged at the tie, the musket went off and he took the shot straight in the mouth. He fell down but got up quickly and started running away. Then he saw that Baboon had fainted clean away and so he hauled his unconscious friend to a nearby water furrow, hoping to throw the farmer's dogs off the scent of the blood running out of his mouth. Aardvark still has no teeth and the mere sight of a gun frightens Baboon witless to this day.

After the episode with the musket, the two friends thought

it best to focus on getting their sheepskin disguises instead. Their search was soon rewarded and they had two that were a perfect fit. In the late afternoon they found themselves being herded along with the sheep into the kraal, according to plan.

At the entrance to the kraal the farmer was counting the sheep. Once the flock was inside, he said to the shepherd: "There are two extra sheep today. I noticed two strange sheep among the flock as I was counting; let's find them."

It wasn't long before the two odd-looking sheep were found. The farmer knew at once who the imposters were, but all he said was: "Tie these two sheep to the gate post. They look sick. I'll bring them some milk to make them feel better."

The farmer returned, not with milk, but with his sjambok. He gave Baboon and Aardvark a sound beating and said: "Leave them tied up here. I have other work to get on with now; I'll deal with them tomorrow."

Night fell and all was quiet. Aardvark accused Baboon of making stupid plans: "And now we're both caught, so there's no way out of this mess for either of us."

Baboon replied: "You're wrong about that, actually. If I were you, we'd have been free ages ago. All you have to do is dig up the gate post so that we can slide the ropes off the bottom."

Amazed that this solution hadn't occurred to him, Aardvark began digging at once and before long the captives were free. Aardvark resolved to give up stealing pumpkins and lambs for evermore and to live on ants instead – they were so much easier to eat – and he decided to become nocturnal so that no one would see his toothless mouth.

Jackal and Wolf build a house

This story highlights Jackal's cunning and Wolf's foolishness.
Wolf is too dim-witted to realise that he is being tricked.

One day when Jackal was visiting, Lion's wife complained about how dilapidated her house was. There were holes in the roof and the walls were about to fall down, she said, and when it rained she and her children got wet.

Jackal began boasting about all the fine houses he and Wolf had built for the farmer and immediately offered to build her a brand-new rondavel. "After all," he said, "it doesn't look good for the king of the animals to live in a ramshackle house."

"Fine," said Lion. "You and Wolf can build me a new rondavel. I'll pay you in food and I'll deliver it myself each day."

Jackal trotted off to Wolf's house and told him about the deal he'd struck with Lion. Wolf could hardly refuse to help build a house for the king and so he went with Jackal. Lion gave them the day's food and the pair immediately set about gathering rocks for the walls.

They had no sooner begun rolling the first rock when Jackal held up his hand in the air and yelped: "Watch out, Brother Wolf! You rolled the rock right onto my hand!" Quickly he wrapped the 'injury' in some animal skin – now he had an excuse to sit in the shade and watch Wolf work, and to chip in whenever Wolf's building technique wasn't quite to his liking. But the moment he saw King Lion approaching, Jackal leapt up and pretended to be working hard: he would not be entitled to his share of the food otherwise.

When the walls were roof-height, Jackal asked for some axes so that they could chop wood for the rafters. In the woods, however, his 'injury' suddenly played up again and he was obliged to leave all the chopping to Wolf. All he was able to do was to tie the poles into bundles for Wolf to lug, huffing and puffing, back to the building site – although Jackal bravely carried one small bundle.

Once the rafters were in place, Jackal said: "Now we need a couple of scythes so that we can cut grass for the thatch. Luckily my hand has healed, so I'll be able to cut grass like nobody's business – you'll see how an expert uses a scythe!" So the pair set off to gather the grass.

Along the way Jackal boasted about how skilfully he'd once cut wheat for the farmer, and when Wolf wasn't looking, he tossed his scythe into the long grass. Then he pretended to see something frightening in the road ahead and, after putting on a great show of alarm, Jackal exclaimed: "Drat! I got such a fright I dropped my scythe. Brother Wolf, you go and cut grass so long while I look for it. When I find it, I'll cut the rest of the grass myself."

The gullible Wolf did as he was told and worked until the sweat ran down his face. Jackal went and found a shady spot out of sight where he could relax and keep a lookout for their paymaster at the same time.

Jackal only 'found' his scythe once Wolf had already cut all the grass that was needed. He pretended to be disappointed: "Gosh, I was looking forward to doing my share of the cutting … oh, well, let's gather the grass into big bundles so that we don't have to make too many trips back and forth."

They made a massive bundle to shoulder between the two of them. Jackal manoeuvred the bundle in such a way that Wolf was carrying the bulk of the burden, but still he complained that he was carrying most of the weight. Wolf meekly shifted more of the load onto his own back, which meant that Jackal ended up carrying nothing at all.

At last they reached the building site and the thatching could begin. As promised, Lion arrived with their food and Jackal couldn't trick Wolf out of his share this time. He began boasting about what an able team of thatchers he and Wolf made, with Wolf working outside and himself working inside, but Lion interrupted him: "Alright, you old windbag, I'll see whether your deeds match your fine words." Lion was well aware that Wolf would be doing the most important part of the job, as thatching from the outside required the most skill.

After Lion had delivered the next food payment, Jackal said to Wolf: "I've been thinking, Brother, our families have so little to eat that we should save half our food each time to take home at the end of the day."

Wolf agreed and so they put half of each payment aside in a cool place inside the rondavel where it would be out of reach of the flies, or so Jackal claimed. Surreptitiously Jackal ensured that a little more than half of the food was set aside each time.

The two thatchers continued to work, with Jackal indoors and Wolf outside on the roof. From time to time Jackal would climb down, allegedly to look for something on the floor, but actually sneaking a bite from the stash of food. When Wolf asked why he needed to climb down so often, Jackal's excuse was that he'd dropped something or other. On one occasion, however, Wolf noticed Jackal stuffing something into his mouth. "What have you got in your mouth, Brother Jackal?" he asked suspiciously.

Jackal swallowed the stolen morsel quickly and stuck a bit of thatching twine between his teeth. "See for yourself, it's just a piece of twine," he said. Reassured, Wolf carried on working. However, he happened to notice their store of food was not increasing, despite the fact that they set half of each payment aside every time. He decided to keep a closer eye on Jackal, but he couldn't catch him in the act.

On the day that the roof was all but done, except for the cone in the centre of the thatch, Wolf peered through the hole and caught Jackal fiddling with the food again. "I knew it!" shouted Wolf as he watched Jackal putting some meat into his mouth. "You are such a thief!"

Jackal reached for another piece of meat and held it up tauntingly. Quite beside himself with rage, Wolf launched himself through the hole to get at the conniving thief, only to find himself dangling in the air, between heaven and earth. Jackal had deliberately sewn Wolf's tail into the thatch during the last round of thatching and tied the twine securely to a rafter. Wolf dangled upside down, cursing a blue streak at the traitor below.

"Stop that racket, Brother Wolf!" called Jackal. "Do you want the farmer's dogs to come? He passed by here with them only a moment ago!"

But there was no stopping Wolf. While the torrent of abuse rained down on him, Jackal calmly collected all the food and went and hid it in the bushes some distance away. He returned to find Wolf still hanging in mid-air and said in his most apologetic tone: "I am awfully sorry for stitching your tail to the thatch, Brother Wolf! I really didn't do it on purpose. Here, let me help you down."

Jackal took a knife and cut the twine to free Wolf's tail. Wolf crashed down to the ground on his head with such force that he was momentarily dazed. As soon as he recovered his wits, he asked: "Where is the food? I want it this minute!"

"*Excuse me*, Brother Wolf," began Jackal indignantly, "when you wouldn't shut up, I was worried the farmer's dogs would come and eat it all, so I took the food and hid it in a safe place."

"Well, alright, but show me where you've hidden it," said Wolf. Off they went to find the food. They searched high and low – everywhere except in the actual hiding place.

At last Jackal exclaimed: "You see! The dogs have taken it because of the ruckus you made!"

Disappointed, Wolf went home empty-handed and with a rumbling tummy despite all his hard work. Jackal, however, made a detour to the hiding place on his way home. He and his family had plenty to eat for a good many days afterwards.

Jackal and Crab run a race

This story tells how Crab came to be a freak of nature, with his flat body and pop-out eyes, and we learn that he is at least as smart as Jackal.

One fine day Jackal went to the water hole to drink. There, he encountered Crab and watched in fascination as the funny little fellow walked backwards, forwards and sideways. Annoyed at being stared at, Crab burst out: "Don't you have any manners? Has no one told you it is rude to stare?"

Never at a loss for words, Jackal retorted: "I'm just amazed that anyone can be so lazy that they can't even be bothered to turn around when they want to change direction. You are the laziest creature I've ever seen!"

"Oh, I get it – you're jealous! That's why you call dexterity laziness! Come on, Mr Pointy Snout, let's see if you can do it," said Crab pretentiously.

"Please! There's nothing to it! I can walk backwards, forwards and sideways without turning my head. In fact, I can probably do it better than you can – here, let me show you," boasted Jackal. Walking straight on was no problem, but when it came to walking sideways towards the right, Jackal stumbled, and when he tried going sideways to the left, he ended up in a thorn bush. Crab began to laugh, and when Jackal's attempt at walking backwards landed him squarely in the water, Crab practically split his sides.

Keen to hide his embarrassment, Jackal retorted: "Oh, you also stagger and end up in the water! Anyway, one thing is for sure: I go much faster and straighter than you do when I walk forwards!"

"Not true, old Pointy Snout – I can get from A to B more

directly and more quickly than you could any day of the week. What's more, if you'll race me to that dead tree on the koppie over there, I'll prove it to you," said Crab, brimming with self-assurance.

"I'm not sure whether you're joking or whether you're trying to mock me, but whatever you're doing you have no business talking to Lion's field cornet in that tone of voice," snapped Jackal.

"I say what I mean and I mean what I say," was Crab's smug reply.

"Alright, you little braggart, you're on," said Jackal.

The two competitors took their marks and in the instant that Jackal darted away from the starting line Crab grasped the end of Jackal's tail with one of his pincers. Oblivious of the passenger clinging to his tail, Jackal ran like the wind. After a while he turned abruptly to check on Crab's progress.

But as Jackal executed this about-turn, Crab released his hold and went sailing through the air into the distance up ahead. "Where are you, Crab?" called Jackal, gazing back the way he'd come.

"Over here, in front," answered Crab.

Jackal turned around and sped off towards the dead tree again. As Jackal overtook him, Crab caught hold of the drooping tail once more.

Jackal picked up the pace and did another about-face after a while to check on Crab. Crab let go at the right moment and the momentum carried him through the air so that he landed further on in the road, as planned.

Again Jackal called to Crab, who replied: "You keep looking for me back there when I'm here, ahead of you!"

To his great consternation Jackal saw that this was true. He pulled out all the stops and raced on towards the tree. When

he reached it he made one last, extra-sharp about-face, which sent Crab flying way past the tree.

"Ha! You have run yourself ragged and I'm not even out of breath," taunted Crab.

Jackal couldn't stand being beaten by Crab. "I don't care who you tell that you won this race; I will simply deny it and say that you are a liar," insisted Jackal, burning with shame at the thought that anyone might find out he'd lost.

Now Shrike happened to be sitting in the dead tree all the while and he'd watched the race. "What are you two arguing about?" he enquired pleasantly.

Jackal quickly and hotly denied that the spindly-legged Crab had won the race. Crab listened without saying anything.

"Jackal, you're too out of breath and too far away for me to hear what you're saying," said Shrike. "Come and sit on this termite mound where I can hear you better."

Jackal went and sat on the termite mound, so doing plugging the entrance to a nest that some wasps had built inside the mound. Confronted with this unexpected obstruction, the wasps decided to unblock the entrance by launching a stinging assault on the intruder. Soon Jackal began shifting about uneasily, taking care not to break eye contact with Shrike. From the growing discomfort in his nether regions, he strongly suspected that his woes were about to multiply, but he was determined not to lose face even further.

Shrike, however, knew what was happening because it was precisely what he had intended. He urged the wasps on: "Come on, come on, lads, zap him! Come on, come on, lads, zap him! Zap him! Zap him!"

Although it was almost impossible to sit still, Jackal continued his argument with all the bravado he could muster.

Then Shrike encouraged the wasps again: "Come on, come

on, lads, zap him! Come on, come on, lads, zap him! Zap him! Zap him!"

Finally the hot seat became too hot for Jackal. He took to his heels in a cloud of dust, swatting here and slapping there for all he was worth. He never breathed a word of the race to anyone ever again.

But Crab did not get off scot-free either. Every time he'd gone sailing through the air ahead of Jackal, he smacked down onto the ground so hard that his shell became flatter and flatter and his eyes popped further and further out of his head, which is why he looks so peculiar.

And that is how Jackal met his match, because no one can be top dog all of the time and every dog will have his day.

Giraffe's great escape

In this story we find out why Giraffe has a long neck, a long tongue and short horns. We also learn more about Jackal's cruelty towards Wolf.

One day the farmer decided to dig a pitfall in the track used by the game on his farm. Jackal happened to come along while he was busy digging and asked what he was doing. The farmer preferred to keep Jackal in the dark about his intentions and so he said: "I'm digging a water hole for the game because they muddy the pan that supplies my own drinking water."

Jackal regarded the pit dubiously; it didn't look like a water hole to him. The farmer, noticing Jackal's scepticism, tried a different tack: "Say, Jackal, you and my old grey wolfhound are still at loggerheads, aren't you? If I were you, I'd make tracks because he's around here somewhere."

Jackal had no desire to encounter the wolfhound and so he suddenly remembered an urgent chore he needed to do at home. But Jackal had acquired a useful piece of information and he trotted directly to King Lion to share what he had learned. Lion was interested to hear about the farmer's pitfall and he immediately made a pact with Jackal to hunt there.

Then Jackal went in search of his longsuffering friend, Brother Wolf. That night the two of them made their way to the farmer's pit and found that a springbok had fallen in.

"How can we get it out?" asked Wolf eagerly.

"Ah, I always come prepared, old friend, I've got everything we need," said Jackal. "I found a rig and since you're so strong, we could put you in the harness and then I could help you pull the springbok out."

Jackal quickly fetched the rig and helped Wolf into the harness. Without much help from Jackal, Wolf pulled the springbok out of the pit.

It was barely done when Lion leapt out from his hiding place. "Wait, let me kill it for you!" he roared. He seized the animal by the throat, chased Wolf and Jackal away and summoned his family to come and eat. He saved some of the meat for Jackal according to their pact; Wolf only got some sinews and bones.

While they were looking for somewhere to hide their rig, Jackal pretended to be outraged at Lion for hijacking the springbok.

The next night Jackal and Wolf found a hartebeest trapped in the pitfall. Again Wolf was harnessed in the rig, but a hartebeest is much heavier than a springbok and it took all Wolf's strength to get the big antelope out. With a great deal of straining and huffing and puffing, he finally succeeded.

As before, Lion jumped out from where he'd been hiding and offered to kill the hartebeest. He promptly did so and again appropriated the carcass for himself and his family, taking care to set aside some meat for Jackal. The hapless Wolf had to be satisfied with the bones and sinews.

Jackal put on another display of outrage at Lion for stealing their hartebeest while he and Wolf were hiding the rig.

The following night Jackal and Wolf found a giraffe in the pit.

"At last! Tonight I will surely get a fair share of meat!" exclaimed Wolf joyfully – he was convinced that Lion and his family couldn't possibly eat a whole giraffe by themselves.

Jackal fetched the rig, tied the straps to Giraffe's horns and helped Wolf into the harness. But Wolf heaved so violently that the horns snapped off, which is why Giraffe only has two little stumps on his head today. Jackal then tied the straps around Giraffe's neck and Wolf pulled this way and that, straining with all his might. Giraffe's tongue stretched further and further out of his mouth and his neck grew longer and longer, but Wolf could not get him out of the hole.

Instead of helping Wolf, Jackal shouted: "Come on, Brother Wolf, you're not pulling! I'm doing all the work here!" He pulled a switch off a tree and wacked Wolf smartly across the rump with it.

"Hey! That hurt!" growled Wolf. "Why are you whipping me when I'm pulling as hard as I can? Can't you see I'm doing my best?"

"Of course I'm not whipping you, Brother Wolf! You're getting tangled in the branches and they are snapping back against you," lied Jackal.

Now, the farmer had discovered that Jackal and Wolf were stealing the game from the pitfall at night and so he was hiding nearby. When he jumped out from behind a bush, Jackal fled, leaving Wolf to face the farmer's wrath. Harnessed to the rig that was still tied to Giraffe, Wolf could not escape the punishing blows the farmer was dealing him – until Giraffe made his great escape, that is. Giraffe had managed to haul himself

out of the pit by wrapping his newly elongated neck around a tree trunk and when he made his bid for freedom, he took Wolf along willy-nilly.

Wolf swung high in the air around Giraffe's neck like a weaver bird's nest in a gale. When Giraffe overtook Jackal at a gallop, Jackal shouted: "Lean forward, Brother Wolf! If you lean forward, you will fall out of the harness!"

"Don't talk to me about leaning forward when I can't even tell which way is up!" roared Wolf. "Why don't you just keep your advice to yourself – and I hope you choke on it!"

After covering a good distance at great speed, Giraffe had had enough of the encumbrance around his neck. He lashed out at Wolf with his foreleg which got caught in the rig. The rig broke into a thousand pieces and Wolf hit the ground with a sickening thud.

Free at last!

Illness in the royal household

In this tale Jackal is up to his old tricks again,
getting Wolf into trouble for his own amusement.

One day Jackal was sitting on a ridge watching Wolf steal upon a herd of kudu. Before long Wolf brought one of the calves to the ground and Jackal immediately began scheming how to get some of the kudu meat into his hungry belly.

He had just figured out a plan when Vulture brought him a message from King Lion. One of Lion's children was sick and, as doctor to the royal household, Jackal was summoned at once to attend to the ailing child.

Jackal was not about to let this inopportune summons upset his applecart, however. He pointed to some herbs growing nearby and said to Vulture: "Here are some of the herbs I need, but the rest only grows on the other side of that ridge over there. It will take me a while to go and gather them. Why don't we send Wolf on ahead with these so long and then I will follow with the other herbs as soon as I've got them?"

"Indeed, Doctor, you know best," agreed Vulture.

Just then Wolf came by with the carcass of a strapping kudu calf over his shoulder. With Vulture in tow, Jackal waylaid Wolf and said briskly: "Brother, I have bad news. King Lion's youngster is sick and he has ordered us to the palace immediately – I have to treat the child and you have to assist me."

Wolf turned questioningly to Vulture, who duly confirmed Jackal's story: "Yes, the king summoned both of you and you'd better be quick about it – it doesn't do to keep Lion waiting, as you know."

"How long has the child been sick?" asked Wolf.

Jackal interrupted him impatiently: "Don't waste time with foolish questions! Hurry up and take your meat home and then take these herbs to Lion as quickly as you can. I'm going to pick the rest immediately and bring them as soon as I can."

But Wolf kicked his heels and Jackal dragged his heels: Wolf wanted to eat right away; Jackal wanted to make sure he would eat later. Wolf blinked first – he took the herbs from Jackal and left with kudu calf over his shoulder. At home he gave the carcass to his wife and hurried to Lion with the herbs.

Jackal took his leave of Vulture and went to the other side of the ridge to collect the necessary herbs. He pulled them up by the roots and wrapped them in some paper. He kept one piece of paper that had writing on and went to Wolf's house. When he got there, he gave it to Wolf's wife, saying: "Wolf and I have to go to King Lion, but he was in such a hurry that he forgot to tell you something, so he wrote it down and asked me to give it to you on my way to Lion."

Mrs Wolf took the piece of paper. She inspected the front and the back, she turned it upside down and the right way up. Then she said: "My husband's writing is so untidy it's impossible to read. Can you make out what it says?"

Jackal took the paper and 'read': "Wife, I made a deal with Jackal. Give him half of the kudu calf and he will give us half a zebra later."

Without batting an eyelid, Jackal handed the paper back and added gravely: "Wolf was actually supposed to deliver the meat to my house – that was part of the deal, you understand – but what with the sickness in Lion's family, I'll save him the trouble and quickly drop it off at home myself before I go to Lion."

Mrs Wolf made her displeasure at the deal abundantly clear: "What is that fool thinking by giving away half the meat when his own family is practically starving?" But Jackal cut short

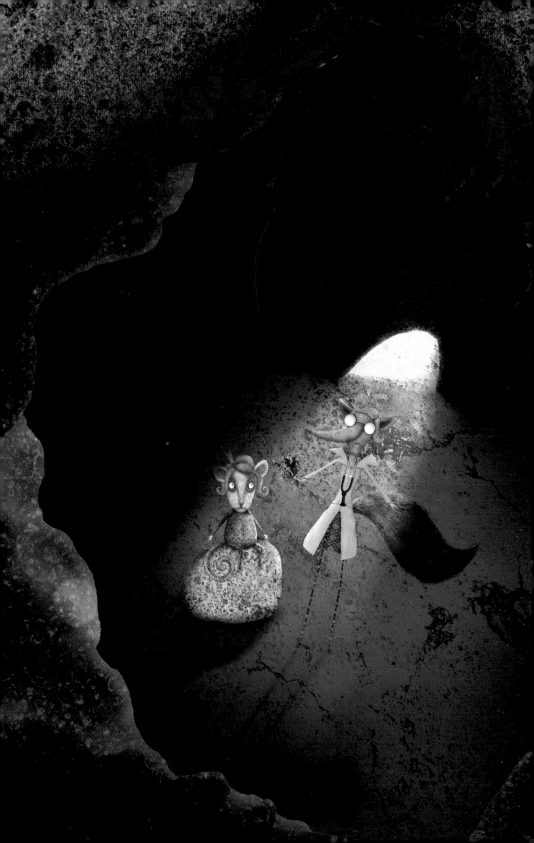

her diatribe against her husband by saying that he was in a tearing hurry and really had to leave that instant.

Mrs Wolf reluctantly handed over half the meat, scolding her absent husband all the while. "Just wait until he gets home," she muttered ominously.

Jackal took the meat, raced home to give it to his wife and finally arrived at Lion's house, out of breath. "What on earth took you so long, Doctor?" roared Lion. "Wolf got here ages ago!"

"Your majesty, I beg your pardon, but the roots of the herbs I needed aren't easy to find. The leaves of the plants are all dried up, you see, and it's a painstaking business to sniff out the roots under the ground," explained Jackal, embroidering inventively.

"Oh, be quiet!" interrupted Lion. "Examine the child and tell me what's wrong with him!"

Jackal put on his most learned face and solemnly poked and prodded the child before pronouncing gravely: "The child has a serious case of inflammation."

Alarmed, Lion asked: "What is the best treatment for inflammation, Doctor?"

"Well," drawled Jackal, "the esteemed doctors who taught me swore by a fresh wolf skin – still warm from the body of the wolf, mind you. Perhaps we could arrange for Wolf's grandmother to be fetched …"

"What? And wait even longer?" interrupted the anxious father. "There's a wolf right here! Grab him and skin him!"

Wolf shot out of the door like a bar of wet soap and raced away with the wind whistling in his ears.

Luckily Jackal's herbal remedies worked, because when Wolf returned with his grandmother on his back, the young lion was up and about and playing outside.

The origins of four kinds of bees

*Honeybee and his daughters belonged to the family of bees
with pale yellow rings around their bodies.*

Honeybee was king of the insects and there were many suitors among his subjects who hoped to win the hand of one of his three daughters. The king decided to hold a banquet so that each daughter could choose her own husband.

The insects accepted the invitation to the banquet eagerly, not only because each hoped to be chosen but also because there would be plenty of honey to eat.

On the day of the banquet, Honeybee called his eldest daughter forward to make her choice. She loved to dance and said her groom would be the one who could dance the longest of all.

The hopeful candidates duly began dancing and flapping their wings. Some danced so exuberantly that they exhausted themselves and dropped out quickly. But Midge was cannier than most. He was also small enough to go unnoticed in the throng. His strategy was to hide away and quickly fly back among the other insects whenever the king called out: "Who isn't tired yet?" Then he'd step forward and show that he wasn't even out of breath. Thus the dancing continued and the aspiring grooms dropped out one by one. At last only Midge remained and could begin his courtship in earnest.

"This is the husband for me," said the eldest royal daughter with satisfaction. "He will be able to work hard and tirelessly."

The other insects were naturally disappointed, but they knew they still had two more chances of being chosen.

Honeybee called upon his second daughter to choose her groom. She wanted a very clever husband and so she said: "I have a question: What is smaller than Midge? Whoever gives the best answer will be the one for me."

The insects were still teasing Midge about being chosen and so one said: "Midge's mouth." Another said: "The food Midge eats." A third said: "The chewed food that Midge swallows."

Then Housefly called out: "The hairs around Midge's mouth, because he doesn't even know when he swallows them."

When no one could give a better answer, Housefly won the hand of the second daughter. The losers were jealous and so they jeered and mocked him, too.

To calm the insects down, the king called out: "There is still one chance left!"

His youngest daughter stepped forward and announced that

she wanted an even cleverer husband than Housefly. The question she asked was: "Who can tell me about something that happened for which no one has ever found an explanation?"

Locust posed the following problem: "An elephant and a midge are standing in the veld, but we can only see the midge."

Dragonfly suggested a solution: "I know why we can't see the elephant! It's because the midge swallowed him!"

Spanish Fly interjected: "I can't see anything! You're all talking nonsense!"

"I know! I know!" shouted Mason Bee excitedly. "When the midge started swallowing the elephant, the elephant began swallowing him back, so they swallowed each other and now there's nothing left to see!"

Mason Bee's reasoning tied everyone up in knots and since no one could think of anything further to say, he won the hand of the youngest daughter.

Midge took his bride home to a hole in a tree trunk, but he knew nothing about making honey. He told his wife: "My honeycombs are only going to have a single layer of cells so that you can see through the combs." He began making a patchwork comb and filled it with honey.

This is how the midget bee came into being. It has no sting and is only slightly bigger than a midge. These little insects live in the warmer northern parts and are particularly bothersome around your face and hands when you perspire.

Housefly couldn't find a nest for his bride and eventually he asked Ant for advice. "The best place for a nest is in the hard ground – you can keep the water out by plastering the inside and the entrance with a patchwork of wax," said Ant. "If you promise to give me some honey, I will show you where you can find an abandoned ant nest."

Housefly agreed on the spot and went off with Ant to find the nest. Then he learned how to make single-layered honeycombs from the little midget bee and filled the patchwork cells with honey. This is how the mocca bee came into being. These bees are the same size as houseflies and they also have no sting. They like living in warm areas. When Ant came round for the honey he'd been promised, Mocca Bee refused. Since then ants have made their nests on bare ground where no grass grows for them to eat.

The history of the mason bee is altogether different. The mason bee is the father of the black bee. Black bees have a sting and they make ferocious use of it. Their honeycombs have a double layer of cells.

When Mason Bee brought his bride home to a small ant

nest in the sand, she said: "Husband, honeybees nest in big holes, not piddling little ones like this." The couple searched until they found a suitable nest in the crags of a mountain. Later, when Mason Bee brought some green leaves in which to store pollen, his wife shook her head: "No, husband, honeybees store honey in wax, not leaves. Go and get some wax."

While he was searching for wax, Mason Bee met Hornet, who said: "Your wife is far too fussy. I use clay and it works just as well."

So Mason Bee took a bit of mud home to his wife. Mrs Mason Bee made it plain that her husband was testing her patience: "I asked for wax, yellow wax. Don't come back without it."

Off the husband went once more. He found some gum and thought it would do. When his wife saw what he'd brought home, she lost her temper and snatched the gum to throw it away. But her paws became stuck to it. Wife and husband yanked and pulled. They twisted and turned and blamed and scolded to no avail – the pair were glued together.

When the shiny black Beetle happened to come by, they asked for his help. Beetle was able to unglue husband and wife, but they never recovered their good humour. To this day they are apt to sting at the slightest provocation, and you are still likely to find black beetles wherever you find mason bees.

Tinktinkie has a party

In this story we learn that size isn't everything and that much can be achieved through cooperation. We read that Tinktinkie considers himself king of the birds and we find out why he sounds the alarm whenever he notices anything out of the ordinary.

There is a lake in a valley on the farmer's property. Birds shelter from the wind and rain and heat in the reeds and bulrushes that grow all around the lake. The farmer's cattle and game go there to drink, and Tinktinkie and Shrew can often be found there, too.

When the other birds spot Tinktinkie at the lake, they invariably tease the tiny bird for fancying himself king of the birds. Shrew also draws teasing comments about his diminutive size from the walking animals at the lake. The two small friends had something else in common: the constant possibility of being killed. The birds were quite prepared to kill Tinktinkie to ensure that he did not become king; and Jackal, Cat, Owl and Hawk were always ready to catch Shrew. Tinktinkie remained cheerful and his bright tinkling song often rang out, 'Tink-tink-tink', but Shrew was reserved and melancholy and so the pair vowed to stand by one another.

One day Tinktinkie was flying around the veld when he encountered Tiger, who asked: "Do the cattle and game still go to the lake to drink?"

"Yes, Uncle Tiger, but you'd better keep away from the farmer's livestock," advised the little bird. Tiger made no answer and so Tinktinkie went on his way.

Tiger chose not to follow the small bird's advice. He lay in wait among the reeds at the lake and attacked the sheep and cattle when they came to drink, leaving many carcasses in his wake.

When Tinktinkie discovered what Tiger had done, he flew straight to the orchard where the farmer was busy clearing the fallen fruit below the trees.

"Ah, Tinktinkie, how is it that the king of the birds flies about all on his own?" asked the farmer, joshing the little bird.

"I am king of the birds," asserted Tinktinkie, "even if none of them wants to accept it. They all want smelly old Vulture to be their king. What has he ever done for them? Nothing! But you could help me and I could be of great service to you in return."

"What could you possibly do for me?" laughed the farmer.

"I can tell you what you don't know," replied Tinktinkie. "Tiger has killed some of your sheep. Wildcat catches your poultry but you don't know where his lair is. Snake kills your brood hens and eats the eggs before you can do anything about it. I can tell you many other things, too. I could also keep the insects that ruin your fruit under control by eating them one by one. And I could call out whenever I see any of the rascals that steal your livestock."

Listening to Tinktinkie, it occurred to the farmer that even small creatures can make a useful contribution and so he said: "What can I do for you?"

Tinktinkie had an answer ready: "Bring the rotten fruit and the dirty grain from your threshing floor to the lake. In return I will eat the pests in your orchard and sound the alarm whenever I see Tiger, Cat or Snake so that you can catch them."

The farmer agreed and did as the little bird asked, and from that day on Tinktinkie has always called out loudly whenever he notices threatening creatures lurking about.

When the farmer had delivered the fruit and grain to the

lake, Tinktinkie told his little friend Shrew: "Now we have plenty of food for the winter. Store enough of the fruit and grain below ground so that you don't have to come out of your nest. I am going to use whatever is left to give the birds a feast." Then Tinktinkie went and spread the word about his feast.

The birds laughed when they heard what Tinktinkie had in mind, but they decided to attend anyway because it would be a good opportunity to make fun of him. When they saw the spread he had laid on, they were astonished. There was grain for the seed-eaters, meat for the carnivores and fruit for the fruit-eaters – even old Vulture found plenty to eat on the sheep carcasses that Tiger had left behind. But still the guests couldn't resist mocking Tinktinkie. "Just because you can provide a feast it doesn't mean you're our equal," they said.

"I will do anything you want me to do, but Vulture won't. You want him to be king but what has he ever done for you? Has he laid on a feast for you? Tell me what you want me to do!" challenged Tinktinkie.

Vulture said nothing because he was wary of the assertive little bird, but Swallow wasn't, and so he said: "You say you can fly higher than any of us, but can you fly further than I can?"

"Let's find out!" retorted Tinktinkie. "I'll race you to that tree at the top of the hill over there and back."

The two flew off, but Tinktinkie quickly took cover in a nearby bush, leaving Swallow to fly on like an arrow from a bow. Tinktinkie's wife happened to be nesting in the tree at the top of the hill and when he saw her there, Swallow as-

sumed it was Tinktinkie himself, so he turned sharply and flew back to the starting point. Of course, when he got there Tinktinkie had already returned, to the utter amazement of the other birds.

One of the songbirds piped up: "Well, I challenge you to a singing contest!" And he began singing so sweetly that the other birds were convinced Tinktinkie had met his match. Not so, however. Tinktinkie took up his fiddle and launched into an entrancing ballad that left the entire audience agape.

Then Peacock stepped forward and said: "Yes, but can you beat me in a plumage contest?"

"Fine!" said Tinktinkie. "But I will wait until winter. Unlike you, Peacock, I don't go about making a spectacle of myself from one minute to the next – no, constancy is my motto." All eyes were on Peacock but he could think of nothing to say.

Mynah stepped quickly into the breach. "Let's see if you can tunnel through the mudbank faster than I can," he challenged.

"You're on!" agreed Tinktinkie, flying straight to the muddy entrance to Shrew's burrow. He scratched open the entrance and came flying out of Shrew's back door almost before Mynah had even begun digging. The baffled birds looked on with growing dismay.

"One thing's for sure," said Duck eager to break the silence, "you couldn't beat me at diving!"

"Well, let's see about that. Let's dive from that side of the mudbank to here," replied Tinktinkie, knowing full well that Shrew's underground passage ran from one side of the bank to the other. Again Tinktinkie was victorious. He emerged from the tunnel, flew up from between the overhanging bulrushes and shook his feathers as if to dry them. The birds were mute with astonishment.

Seriously annoyed by the invincible little upstart, Guinea Fowl was ready to resort to violence. "Let's fight it out then, Tinktinkie!" he challenged.

"Alright, I'm ready for you," said Tinktinkie. He had spotted a supple branch caught behind a sturdier one that he could put to good use: if he were to release the trapped branch, it would snap back and deliver a resounding blow. The canny little bird squared up to Guinea Fowl in such a way that the latter was positioned directly in the path of the branch as it snapped back. The blow sent Guinea Fowl tumbling head over heels. He lay dazed on the ground with his legs in the air.

"Come, Vulture, let's see you do everything I have done," taunted Tinktinkie, puffed up with victory.

Vulture quickly flew away before anyone could tell how daunted he felt. None of Tinktinkie's victories that day convinced anyone to accept him as king of the birds, but he has not given up yet.

Pig looks for his legacy

In this tale we find out why Pig rootles in the dirt and why he lives with humans, and we discover why Dog digs in the ground and why he sometimes twitches and whimpers in his sleep.

Long ago Pig lived in the wild, in forests and ravines. During that time, Lion was crowned king of the animals and he held a banquet to celebrate his coronation. He decided to present gifts and legacies to all the animals who attended the celebration. Pig was also present, but he arrived after all the gifts and legacies had already been handed out.

"Since you have come to acknowledge me as your king, Pig, you too will have a legacy, but you will have to ask the earthworms for it – I gave it to them to keep for you," said Lion.

So Pig went to all the damp places where earthworms lived and immediately began burrowing around with his snout. "Where have you put the legacy Lion gave me and what is it?" he asked the first earthworm he found.

"It is a large wooden bowl that magically fills up with food and water twice a day and we buried it under some root vegetables," replied the earthworm.

Pig went straight to the field where the farmer grew potatoes and sweet potatoes and began snuffling in the ground.

He found plenty to eat, but he did not find his wooden bowl. "Where have you buried the legacy that Lion gave you to keep for me?" he asked an earthworm in the potato field.

The earthworm directed him to the farmer's pumpkin patch. "It is buried among those big leaves over there," said the earthworm.

Pig bit chunks out of the pumpkins to see if they weren't perhaps his magic bowl. He did not find his legacy, but he managed to have a good meal nonetheless. "Have you seen my food bowl?" he asked an earthworm in the pumpkin patch.

"The last time I saw it, it was lying under those sheaves over there," said the earthworm.

Pig went and rummaged among the sheaves. He found more food, but no sign of his bowl. When the farmer saw Pig rootling among the sheaves he walked over and said: "Tell me, old Bottlenose, why are you wrecking my vegetable patches and sheaf stacks?"

Pig explained that Lion had given his legacy to the earthworms for safekeeping, but the earthworms were sending him from pillar to post and he couldn't find his magic bowl anywhere.

"Ah, I know where it is," said the farmer. "It got washed up during the heavy rain and ended up buried in the mud behind the field over there. Go and look in the mud and you'll find it."

Pig hunted all over in the mud. He found – and ate – lots of pondweed, but he did not find his bowl. Dejected, he flopped down in the mud. After a while he decided to go and see if the farmer couldn't shed more light on his elusive legacy.

In the meantime, the farmer had built a pigpen out of wooden poles and placed a food bowl inside. When Pig came back and began asking about the bowl that filled up with food and water in the morning and evening, the farmer said: "Oh, now I know which bowl you're talking about. I call it a trough. Come, I'll show you where it is."

Pig followed the farmer into the pigpen. He walked over to the trough of food and water and started eating. "At last I've found my legacy!" he exclaimed between mouthfuls.

Pig was in clover. Twice a day the trough was filled with food and water which meant he didn't have to look for food anymore. He could spend the day plotting his revenge on the earthworms instead – Pig still eats any earthworms he comes across.

Dog, however, was not as well fed as Pig; he had to be satisfied with scraps from the farmer's table. He watched enviously as Pig grew stouter by the day and eventually he said: "What if you and I were to swap places for a while, Pig? You could guard the farmyard and I could guard your legacy, then I might also put some meat on my bones."

Pig agreed to this proposal because he sometimes got bored with nothing to do in the pigpen all day long. So the two changed places and when the farmer asked why Pig was wandering around the farmyard, he explained that he and Dog had swapped places. The farmer listened to the explanation without a word.

Dog lay in the pigpen dreaming about legacies. He dreamt that Hare stole the legacy and buried it in a mouse hole. To this day, when you see Dog twitching and yelping in his sleep, he is dreaming of Hare carrying away the legacy and he looks for it by digging open mouse holes.

One day the farmer and his wife came to the pigpen and found Dog lying inside. With a twinkle in his eye, the farmer said loudly to his wife: "I reckon Dog is fat enough to be slaughtered now. We need to go and boil some water so long so that we can scrape off his fur."

The farmer and his wife had no sooner left the pigpen when Dog leapt out and hurried off to find Pig. "It's time for you to guard your legacy again, Pig," he said. "I'd rather guard the farmyard than lie around getting fat."

Pig needed some convincing and so dog had to drag him into the pigpen by the ear. As for Dog, he steered clear of the pigpen from that day on and never slept in it again.

Aardvark's missing tooth ointment

*This tale tells why Aardvark digs for ants, why Baboon never
hides in holes, and why Aardvark and Jackal share burrows.*

Aardvark and Baboon were old friends even though it was
Baboon's fault that Aardvark lost all his teeth in an un-
fortunate encounter with a steel trap. When Lion heard about
Aardvark's misfortune, he sent the ants with some special ointment to make Aardvark's teeth grow again. Somehow the ants
and the aardvark never managed to meet up and the delivery
of the ointment was indefinitely delayed.

One day Baboon found Aardvark furiously excavating an
anthill. "Say, old friend, you're digging away like someone in
a temper and the day has hardly even begun," said Baboon.

"Well, I **am** cross and I'll stay cross until I find the blasted
ants who were supposed to bring me the ointment Lion sent
to make my teeth grow again. You remember how I lost them
all in that trap, don't you?" grunted Aardvark as he sent clods
of earth flying in every direction.

"Erm, yes," said Baboon, quickly offering to help look for
the ants to show what a good friend he was. He immediately
began scratching in the dirt and peering under stones, but he

was really only helping himself – he liked eating the bulbs in the ground and the insects under the stones.

After the two animals had been working in silence for some time Baboon said: "My friend, I think we're barking up the wrong tree here. Yesterday I heard a rumour that your special ointment has been buried near the farmer's fruit orchard. Have you looked there yet? If I were you, I'd go and look there to-night. But you must be sure to dig down far into the ground, because, according to the rumour, the calabash with the oint-ment is buried quite deep." And with that, Baboon sat down on a rock and folded his arms across his bulging belly.

Aardvark decided to take Baboon's advice. He stopped dig-ging and went home – after all, it was time for nocturnal ani-mals like him to be asleep.

The next morning when Baboon crept up to the orchard, he found Aardvark there and he was pleased to see the deep holes his friend had dug during the night – deep holes made excel-lent hiding places when the farmer and his dogs came by! Baboon snuck into the orchard, climbed a tree and picked an armful of fruit. As he was climbing down again, the farmer and his dogs appeared.

Aardvark and Baboon scampered into one of the holes, be-lieving they'd be safe inside. But the dogs were soon nosing their way into the hole and Aardvark had to dig for all he was worth from the inside to block the opening.

Baboon began to suspect that he'd landed them in a bit of a pickle. They were trapped in a hole in the ground with no way out except into the dogs' eager jaws – and what was more, all his fruit lay buried somewhere under the sand. The situa-tion was dire and it soon got worse. The farmer brought a pick and shovel and began digging from above. All Aardvark could do was to dig down even further.

As Aardvark dug furiously downwards, the loosened stones pelted Baboon on the head and chest. He could hardly see or breathe for all the sand flying about in the tight space. All he could do was grunt whenever a stone found its target.

When it grew dark the farmer gave up since it was clear that the two animals were simply tunnelling further and further down – tomorrow was another day after all.

In the dead of night Aardvark tunnelled to the surface and they were free at last. He stormed off to resume his search for the ants and the ointment, cursing Baboon as he went. Unsurprisingly, their friendship did not survive the ordeal and Baboon thought twice about hiding in holes in the future.

Sometime afterwards, Jackal found Aardvark digging a hole under an anthill. Jackal considered himself an expert on the subject of holes – they could be homes or hideouts, depending on the circumstances – and so he decided it might be worthwhile cultivating Aardvark's acquaintance. "Excuse me, friend, may I ask if you're still looking for the tooth ointment that Lion asked the ants to give you?" began Jackal by way of introduction.

"I am. I can't chew properly without teeth," snapped Aardvark.

"Well, you can stop searching because I am Lion's doctor and I made the tooth ointment for the king. I'll gladly make you some more if you collected the ingredients – all I need is honey, an ostrich egg and donkey milk," said Jackal, listing some of his favourite things to eat.

"But where will I find the ingredients?" asked Aardvark eagerly.

"I'll show you, but you must gather them yourself because it will increase the potency of the ointment," replied the wily jackal.

First he led Aardvark to a beehive for the honey, taking care to stand well back as Aardvark went to work. The bees were not about to relinquish their honey without a fight and they stung Aardvark mercilessly. From time to time he had to retreat, but eventually he managed to extract a comb. He put it in a calabash and took it to Jackal.

Jackal inspected the honey for a moment and then said: "I'm afraid this isn't the right kind of honey. We need the honey made by the African bee." He ate the 'wrong' honey first and then led Aardvark to a hive of African honeybees. Before Aardvark had even reached the hive, a horde of worker bees responded to the threat of an intruder by attacking him aggressively. When Aardvark set to work on the hive itself, things became positively dire, but somehow he persevered and managed to extract a few honeycombs.

Jackal sniffed the combs, turning them this way and that. Then he said: "Well, this is the right kind of honey, but some of the combs are not up to scratch, so I won't be able to use them all."

He licked the fat honeycombs until they were practically empty, then he set them aside and said: "Come with me; I'll show you where to find ostrich eggs." Jackal led the way to a nest of ostrich eggs and took up his position in the safety of a nearby ditch.

Aardvark stormed the nest. The ostriches lashed out with their feet, leaving red welts all over his body. Aardvark was not deterred by the ferocious kicks, however; he doggedly rolled an egg to the ditch where Jackal was hiding and pushed it over the edge. Then he went back to the nest to get another one. The ostriches kicked him to within an inch of his life.

When Aardvark eventually took cover in the ditch, he found Jackal holding an empty ostrich egg – he said it broke when

Aardvark pushed it into the ditch, and since the shell was useless, they'd have to come back and try again later once the ostriches had calmed down.

Jackal decided the ostriches had settled down sufficiently when he felt like eating another egg. As it turned out, the big birds were anything but calm and Aardvark suffered the full force of their parental anger.

Jackal's explanation for the second empty eggshell was that it had also broken when Aardvark pushed it into the ditch. He used the same ruse several times more before he suggested that they could go and get the donkey milk first.

He led Aardvark to a jenny that was grazing in the veld with her foal. Needless to say the mother donkey did not take kindly to giving up her milk – she kicked Aardvark until he saw stars.

Jackal never got round to making the special tooth ointment, but he and Aardvark still sometimes share a burrow. As for Aardvark, he hasn't stopped looking for the ants and his ointment.

Jackal and the tiger skins

In this tale we discover why Tiger always surges forward when someone grabs him by the tail, why he avoids steep cliffs and how he got the markings on his coat.

Tiger had been out for revenge ever since Jackal ate his cubs, but the clever Jackal always managed to keep out of his way – until one particular day.

Jackal and Vulture were old friends and when Vulture told Jackal where Tiger usually spent part of the day, Jackal decided to settle the matter with his enemy once and for all. At the very edge of Vulture Crag there grew a tree, explained Vulture, and it was to this tree that Tiger came early each morning. First Tiger would sharpen his claws on the trunk and then he'd climb the tree and settle down for a nap on a particular branch that extended over the rocky ledge.

Jackal went to inspect the tree when he knew Tiger wouldn't be around and, sure enough, there were the claw marks on the tree trunk and there was the overhanging branch. Jackal realised that if the branch were to be weakened somehow, it would break when Tiger lay on it and then he'd plunge into the abyss below. So Jackal searched for a sharp stone that would serve as a saw. He was busy sawing the underside of the branch when Vulture arrived.

"What are you doing, my friend?" asked Vulture.

"Oh, I'm just planning ahead," replied Jackal meaningfully.

The next morning Tiger returned to the tree as usual. He sharpened his claws on the trunk and then climbed up to the branch for his nap. He'd no sooner settled down when the branch broke beneath his weight with a resounding Crack! Tiger tumbled head over heels off the cliff. His fall was broken by a rocky ledge below and he found himself lying on a narrow lip where the vultures were nesting.

The birds quickly tackled him. One grabbed him by the scruff of his neck, another took hold of his tail and others gripped any part of him within their reach. They flew up into the air over the sheer drop and then let go. Tiger landed squarely on his feet as cats are apt to do, but he was embarrassed nonetheless. He suspected that Jackal was ultimately behind his ignominious plunge to the ground and he resolved to hunt him down.

On a cold day Tiger spotted Jackal warming himself by a fire in the lee of a mountain. Tiger stole up on him and pounced, but Jackal leapt nimbly aside, simultaneously grabbing a burning log with one hand and Tiger's tail with the other. Jackal walloped his captive all over and when Tiger turned towards him, Jackal thrust the glowing log into his face so that Tiger's only option was to surge forward mightily in an effort to escape. Then Jackal suddenly let go of Tiger's tail and scarpered up the mountain. To this day Tiger's coat bears the scorched striped pattern and he can't stand anything holding onto his tail.

Tiger saw Jackal on a ridge above him and set off in pursuit, but Jackal called out: "If you follow me up here, Tiger, I'll set my dogs on you."

"I've taken on the farmer's great big dogs singlehandedly, so I'm not scared of your little mutts!" retorted Tiger.

Jackal rolled a rock down the cliff, shouting: "Go, Storm! Go and get him!" But Tiger stepped aside and the rock bounded past.

"Your little cur is all bark and no bite, Jackal! See how it runs away!" called Tiger.

In reply Jackal pushed two rocks down the cliff, shouting: "Go, Fang! Go, Jaws! Tear that tiger to shreds!"

But the two rocks crashed past on either side of Tiger without doing any harm. "Look at the cowards fleeing with their tails between their legs!" he taunted.

Jackal shoved three rocks down the cliff, shouting: "Go, Bounder! Go, Prancer! Go, Springer! Tear that tiger limb from limb!"

Three rocks proved too much for Tiger, however. Prancer crashed into his chest, knocking the breath out of him and sending him reeling. When he recovered his wits, he threw in the towel (and he has avoided steep cliffs ever since), but not without a great deal of bluster about what he'd do to Jackal the next time their paths crossed.

Jackal was secretly relieved to have time out and decided to make himself scarce. But when Tiger saw Jackal near a water hole one day, he crept up on his old foe.

Jackal realised he'd been cornered and he had to think quickly, so he stared fixedly into the water, pawing the surface from time to time.

Tiger wondered what he was up to. "Now I've got you!" shouted Tiger. "What are you doing here and what are you staring at?"

Without looking up, Jackal replied: "I'm soaking the skins of all the tigers I've killed."

"You're lying!" roared Tiger.

"Don't take my word for it," said Jackal. "Come and see for yourself."

He stepped back to let Tiger look into the water and while Tiger stood mesmerised by the image reflected back at him, Jackal slipped away.

Tiger stared and stared at the skin in the water and eventually reached out a paw to touch it. In that instant he realised it was his own reflection and not the skin of another tiger at all. He spun round to deal with Jackal, but of course he wasn't there.

He raced after Jackal, who saw him coming. Luckily, Jackal found a dead elephant nearby. He leapt on top of the carcass and adopted the pose of a triumphant elephant hunter. "Ah, there you are, Tiger. Give me a hand, won't you? I've just killed this elephant and I want to skin it."

The scene before his eyes gave Tiger pause for thought. He turned and walked away as if he had far more important things on his mind, leaving the phoney elephant killer without an audience.

Where Turtle came from

*In this tale we discover when Raven learned to talk; why Duck and Goose poke
their heads under the water; why Turtle bobs up and down and likes to catch
ducklings and goslings.*

The farmer was walking by the river one day when he saw
a raven's nest in a tree. He climbed up to look and found
two fledglings that were just about ready to leave the nest. He
decided to take the young birds home to his children.

The children were delighted with their new pets and taught
them to talk and say funny things. The talking ravens were a
great favourite, until they developed a liking for shiny objects.
The farmer's spectacles went missing, so did his wife's teaspoons and some of the children's buttons.

But that was not the worst of it. When the ravens were heard
saying rude words, the farmer decided they would have to
go. He did not want to kill them, however, because they didn't
know it wasn't nice to swear and so he simply chased them
away with the warning that he would shoot them if they returned to the farmyard.

The ravens left and went back to their old nest, where they
reproached the farmer noisily.

Tortoise was passing by and heard the cacophony. He asked
what had upset the ravens. They explained that the farmer
had banned them from the farmyard because they'd taken
some shiny things to play with and put them in the woodpile
– and because they'd learnt to say rude words.

Tortoise nodded sagely. "I'm free to come and go because I
don't take things that aren't mine, and I never get into argu-
ments because I don't talk. If I were to make things right be-

tween you and the farmer, what will you do for me?" he asked.

"We'll teach you to fly," chorused the ravens.

"Teach me to fly? That sounds unlikely, but let me go and negotiate with the farmer first. I'll come back to tell you how it went," said Tortoise, setting off at once.

He eventually arrived at the farmyard well after dark and made his way to the woodpile where he found the ravens' treasure-trove. Painstakingly he carried the spectacles, the teaspoons, a small pair of scissors, some buttons and several other shiny objects across the farmyard and laid them at the kitchen door. Then he crept back and hid in the woodpile so that he could observe what would happen next.

The farmer opened the kitchen door the following morning and found all the missing items. He felt bad about accusing the ravens when it seemed all too likely that his children had taken the objects and left them lying about. After the father had scolded the children and they'd all gone back into the house, Tortoise left the woodpile and headed for the river.

The ravens weren't at their nest when he arrived, so he wandered along the riverbank, looking for somewhere to cross – the grass was ever so much greener on the other side and tender green grass was what Tortoise liked best.

When the ravens returned, Tortoise related the events at the farmyard which suggested that the farmer no longer blamed them and that they were free to go back there. The birds were delighted and asked what they could do for Tortoise in return.

Tortoise explained that he could find no way of crossing the river to the lush green grass on the opposite bank.

"Well, we promised to teach you to fly, but we can get you to the other side by other means as well," offered the ravens. "Each of us will hold one end of a stick in our beaks while you hold on to the middle. That way we could carry you across the river."

Tortoise considered this a satisfactory plan and in no time the ravens were conveying him through the air.

Fish caught sight of the three when they were about half-way across the river. "Come and look! Come and look!" he called to the other creatures in the river. "Tortoise is flying and he doesn't even have wings! What a sight for sore eyes!"

Tortoise ignored the gibe and simply gripped the stick more firmly in his beak.

"Oh my goodness!" laughed Crab. "Old Tortoise is a wing-less wonder!"

Tortoise did not deign to answer him either.

Then Frog, who was an altogether more polite animal, called out a greeting: "Good morning, Grandpa! How are you today?"

"Good morning, my boy!" was all Tortoise managed to say before he hit the water with a Splash! Being quite a heavy animal, he sank rapidly beneath the water – and there he has remained ever since, under the name of Turtle.

Fish, Crab, Eel and Frog discovered it was rather pleasant having a new neighbour and they quickly showed Turtle the ropes. Unlike many of them, however, he preferred not to spend all his time in the water and so he crawled out onto the riverbank occasionally to bask in the sun. It also seemed more sensible to him for turtles to lay their eggs in the warm sand where they would hatch more easily. And when the baby turtles emerged from their shells, they would be a stone's throw from the water after all.

One day Turtle and his brood were dozing in the sunshine on the riverbank. Duck and Goose and their respective young-sters also liked to nap on the riverbank, but the ducklings and

their little cousins never slept for very long and when they woke up, they made a great deal of noise. This annoyed Turtle and he gave them a severe telling-off.

Duck and Goose did not like having their children scolded by anyone else and they retaliated by pecking the baby turtles. In the argument that followed, everyone ended up in the water and Turtle and his brood dived beneath the surface.

Duck and Goose were not about to let Turtle off that lightly. They kept sticking their heads under the water to look for the turtle family, who in turn bobbed up from time to time to see what the water birds were doing. This curious behaviour continues to this day and adult ducks, geese and turtles think nothing of eating one another's young when they get the chance.

Little Jackal and little Wolf

This tale is about the mischief children get up to
and how to catch them out.

Jackal and Wolf use to be hard-working once. They grew fruit and vegetables and each of them built a wattle-and-daub hut for their families to live in. Jackal had a young son and so did Wolf. The two striplings were lively and full of mischief. They liked to play in a nearby clay pit where they made oxen out of the abundant supply of pale clay.

Mrs Jackal and Mrs Wolf both kept ducks that could often be found in the water at the clay pit, but the duck-breeding wasn't going very well. When the mothers asked the two boys why there were hardly any eggs or ducklings, the youngsters said Otter was stealing them. The mothers accepted their sons' explanation; the fathers were dubious but they kept their doubts to themselves.

Come suppertime, both boys had little appetite for their mothers' food – they'd eaten too many of their clay oxen, they said. Jackal and Wolf decided to put this likely story to the test and the next day they asked the boys to show them the so-called edible clay. But the boys claimed that there wasn't any left.

It so happened that the ducks had also stopped laying just then and there were no ducklings either, so the youngsters had to look elsewhere for something to eat. Their fathers' sweet potato plots provided a solution and the boys carried armfuls of sweet potatoes to the clay pit, where they made a fire and baked them in the hot ash.

When they noticed someone had been digging up their

sweet potatoes, Jackal and Wolf conferred and decided to question their sons. The boys accused Porcupine of the theft.

That night the young wolf and the young jackal were too full to eat supper again. They said they'd found more of the edible clay and they'd eaten too many of their special clay oxen. Jackal and Wolf conferred once more and the next day they said to their sons: "Show us these clay oxen that you like eating so much."

The boys trotted ahead to the clay pit and when they got there, each of them promptly ate a clay ox. Jackal picked up one of the 'delicacies' and broke it open. It turned out to be a baked sweet potato covered in a thin layer of clay. Wolf followed Jackal's example and also found a baked sweet potato inside. The fathers just shook their heads. They went home, dug up all the remaining sweet potatoes and stored them out of reach of the two mischief-makers.

Round about the same time, the quinces began ripening and when Jackal and Wolf inspected their trees, they noticed that the fruit was disappearing day by day. After discussing the matter, Jackal and Wolf asked their boys if they knew what might have happened to the quinces. Baboon was the thief, said the boys. Another likely story, thought the fathers, but they said no more about it.

Again the youngsters had no appetite for supper that night, owing, they said, to the masses of edible clay they'd found. Again the Jackal and Wolf kept their sceptical opinions to themselves. All they asked was to be shown this new discovery of clay that was good enough to eat.

At the clay pit the following day, the boys each tucked into a clay ox with relish. "Show us how you make them," asked the incredulous fathers. "We'd like to see how you do it."

The boys were happy to demonstrate and soon held up two finished clay oxen. When their fathers broke them open, however, there were no baked quinces inside. So they offered the oxen to the boys to eat. "They aren't ready yet," explained the boys. "They have to stand for a day before we can eat them." Jackal and Wolf shook their heads and went home to get on with their chores.

That afternoon Mrs Jackal and Mrs Wolf asked their sons to take some lunch to their fathers. The boys dutifully took the food and the two calabashes of milk, but they made a detour to the clay pit first. There, each one found a secluded spot behind some bulrushes and got up to mischief the nature of which remained a secret. All we know is that the fathers complained that the milk was thin and watery by the time it reached them.

When Jackal and Wolf took up the matter of the watery milk with their wives that night, the women were perplexed. "The milk was rich and creamy when I poured it into the calabash," said each wife. A whispered conversation followed between the parents, which the sons could not overhear.

The next day the youngsters had to take lunch to their fathers again, but before they set off, each mother told her son privately: "I'm going to rub some clay on your lips so that your father can tell whether you've been drinking the soup in the calabash." Then she dipped a finger into some clay, but she did not rub that finger over her son's lips; she used a clean finger instead. Unaware of what had happened at each other's houses, the boys departed with the food.

Again they made a detour to the clay pit where they proceeded to do to the soup what they had done to the milk the day before. When they had finished, each one secretly 're-applied' some clay to his lips and then they set off together.

Jackal and Wolf inspected the soup and asked straight away why it was so watery. The boys said their mothers had given it to them like that. "So you didn't drink any of it and then fill the calabashes with water?" queried the fathers. The boys insisted they had not and pointed to the clay on their lips as proof of their innocence. The fathers explained why the clay was in fact proof of exactly the opposite before marching their sons over to where two switches, newly plucked from a tree, lay waiting. What happened next is easy to guess.

Back among their quince trees, Jackal and Wolf picked all but a couple of quinces and stored the fruit out of their sons' reach.

The youngsters spent the following day at the clay pit as usual, but came running home in the evening, yelping and howling and rubbing their mouths – much to the amusement of their fathers and the concern of their mothers.

For some reason the clay oxen had been anything but tasty that day – in fact, it felt as if they'd set their mouths on fire, explained the wailing boys.

The fathers wondered aloud whether the fiery treats had anything to do with the last two quinces which were now missing and which had been stuffed with chili. The boys denied any knowledge of the missing fruit, but the fiery quinces would not be denied.

The young jackal and the young wolf continued playing in the clay pit. They made many clay oxen, none of which were for eating, because all the edible clay was forever used up – or so they said.

Jackal, Wolf and the overhanging rock

The events in the following tale took place after Wolf had endured many years of suffering at Jackal's hands. Wolf had finally resolved to do away with his torturer and was constantly on the lookout for the right opportunity, even while he was out hunting.

One day Jackal was walking in a long narrow ravine. The sun was hot and he decided to rest a while in the shade of an overhanging rock. He'd no sooner flopped down beneath the rocky ledge when he saw Wolf entering the ravine from the opposite end. Escape was not an option and so Jackal quickly leapt up onto his hind legs, pressed his front paws up against the overhanging rock and held the pose.

Wolf couldn't believe his luck when he saw Jackal in what was a clearly vulnerable position. "Now I've got you!" shouted Wolf. "Today is the day you meet your end and I will show not a jot of mercy!"

As Wolf began his menacing approach, Jackal said: "Honestly, Brother Wolf, this is not the place to pick a fight! I'm having all my days holding up this rock and if you tackle me now, I'll have to let go and then we'll both be crushed! Is that what you want? To be squashed into oblivion?"

Wolf eyed the rock. It was protruding rather precariously and it wasn't inconceivable that Jackal was all that was holding it up. But Wolf was so consumed with rage that he said: "No, you dirty scoundrel, that's just another one of your tall stories. Get ready to meet your end!"

With a last glance at the rock, Wolf charged. As he reached out to grab hold of his old enemy, Jackal yelled: "That's it! I'm letting go! See you in the next world!"

Wolf panicked. What if Jackal was telling the truth for once? The possibility won out over his desire for revenge. He leapt onto his hind legs and thrust his paws up to support the rock. Jackal jumped aside and watched Wolf straining upwards beneath the rock. Considering it unwise to antagonise Wolf just then, Jackal said in his most encouraging voice: "Hold on, Brother Wolf. Hold on for a bit longer while I run home for an axe. I'll chop down that sturdy tree trunk over there and use it to support the rock once and for all. Whatever you do, don't let go until I get back!"

"I won't," grunted Wolf, "Just hurry up, will you?"

"I'll be back before you know it," promised Jackal as he trotted away. Of course, nothing could have been further from the truth.

Wolf stretched up for all he was worth. He soon grew tired and wished he could use his shoulder to prop up the rock, but it was too high.

Hours became days and there was no sign of Jackal. Hunger, thirst and exhaustion overtook Wolf, but he held on steadfastly.

Vulture alighted nearby and regarded the spectacle. When he heard Jackal's part in it, he decided not to inform Wolf that the rock was, in fact, securely anchored to the cliff and had no chance of falling down. Jackal had helped Vulture in his bid to become king of the birds, after all, so Vulture flew away without ending Wolf's misery.

Egret had also noticed Wolf's on-going tribulation and he came to find out what was going on. Wolf explained that he'd finally caught up with Jackal when he found him holding up the rocky ledge and was all set to kill the rascal for the misery he had caused over the years. "But then he threatened to let go, so now I'm holding it up until Jackal brings an axe to make

a support. I can't let go without being squashed as flat as a pumpkin leaf."

"And you took Jackal at his word?" asked Egret incredulously. "My dear chap, that rock has hung there like that for years and years! Believe me, you can let go; it is firmly attached to the cliff. Besides, Jackal isn't coming back – I heard him boasting about planting you under this ledge forever. If you don't let go, you'll die and your skeleton will be left standing here to remind everyone of the last trick Jackal played on you."

Wolf gazed up at the rock for a while, but then he shook his head and said: "No, Egret, I'm not willing to take the chance. I'm going to wait for Jackal to come."

"So, you'll take his word over mine?" interrupted Egret. "When I'm being honest with you and he has lied to you so many times in the past?" Egret shook his feathers and tried again. "Why don't you try letting go with one paw first? If nothing happens then you know I'm telling the truth."

Gingerly Wolf took one paw off the rock, but almost immediately put it back again – he was so lightheaded with hunger and fatigue that he thought he saw the rock move.

Egret finally lost patience with Wolf. "How can you be so stupid?" he shouted. "The rock didn't move! Let go and jump out from under it, you fool!"

Galvanised by Egret's insults, Wolf let go and fled. He ran all the way home without a backward glance.

Exhausted and traumatised by his experience, Wolf was unable to give his wife and mother a sensible account of where he'd been all that time. Nor did his haggard emaciated appearance soften their hearts. The two irate females hounded him straight out of the door with brandishing broomsticks and burning logs. "And don't dare come back without food again!" they scolded.

Jackal, Wolf and the hot rock

Jackal has to keep his wits about him if he is to avoid Wolf,
who is out for revenge now more than ever.

Jackal had the habit of taking his prey to a particular spot from where he had a clear view of the surrounding area, so that he could eat without being caught unawares. The feathers, claws and paws of many previous catches lay on the ground around him.

Jackal had just arrived at his special vantage point when he saw Wolf catching a hare in the distance. He watched as Wolf caught another hare and stuffed both of them into what looked like a brand-new knapsack. But then Wolf turned and began heading straight towards Jackal who was not inclined to beat a retreat just then.

Quickly he snatched up his worn old knapsack and filled it with stones and grass. On top he added a layer of partridge feathers and guinea-fowl wings. He pushed a couple of rabbit paws and bird claws through the holes in the bag. When he was done, it looked as if his knapsack was bursting at the seams with game and birds.

He tossed the heavy knapsack over his shoulder and walked jauntily to meet Wolf. He shouted a greeting as he approached and began boasting about how successful his hunting had been that day. "Ah, Brother Wolf, I have wreaked havoc among the hares, partridges and guinea fowls this morning! Have you also had good hunting?"

"What I have and haven't caught is none of your business," snarled Wolf.

"Come now, Brother Wolf, that's no way to respond to a friendly enquiry," said Jackal, sounding hurt. "What good does it do to bear a grudge against someone who has been your friend since childhood? The course of friendship is not always smooth and I have as much to complain about as you do, you know. Why don't we make amends? It would be such a shame to grow old as enemies, don't you think?"

The warmth and apparent sincerity of Jackal's words had the desired effect on Wolf's resolve and before long the pair were reminiscing amiably about the good old days. From time to time Jackal drew attention to his bulging knapsack and brought the conversation round to the successful hunting he'd enjoyed that morning. It wasn't hard to convince Wolf that the bag was filled with game and birds.

Suddenly Jackal groaned and put a paw to his chest. "What a dreadful pain," he gasped. "I think I'd better go home, Brother, I don't feel well at all." He got up and reached for his knapsack, but pretended to struggle under its weight. "Would you mind carrying this heavy bag part of the way for me, old friend? I'll carry yours and then we can swop up ahead."

Wolf picked up Jackal's tatty old bag and found that it was very heavy indeed. He grumbled as he slung it over his shoulder, but reasoned privately that it would be no great loss if Jackal ran off with his new knapsack – Jackal's bag definitely contained much more than two hares!

They walked past a crevice in some rocks which Jackal had put to good use many times before and this time it was no different. Whoosh! He slipped into the narrow passage like a bar of wet soap and began laughing scornfully at Wolf.

"You can laugh as much as you like," retorted Wolf. "I've got all your game and you've only got my two hares!"

Then he went on his way. He knew Jackal had enough to

eat for a couple of days so there was little point in waiting him out.

Wolf arrived home and cheerfully handed the knapsack over to his wife and mother. They were pleasantly surprised by its promising weight, but their mood changed rapidly as they unpacked a heap of stones, grass, feathers, paws and claws.

"Where's my new knapsack?" bellowed old Mother Wolf. "What a useless son you are!"

"What am I going to feed these hungry children?" shouted Mrs Wolf. "What a useless husband and father you are!"

Biff! Bash! The two angry females shoved Wolf out the door amid a flurry of blows.

It is no surprise that Wolf was filled with a black hatred towards Jackal, and Jackal knew in his heart of hearts that he'd probably played his last trick on Wolf.

That night Jackal was so deep in thought that his wife, oblivious of his latest treachery towards Wolf, asked: "Is something troubling you, dear? Has something happened? You don't usually let things upset you."

Jackal sighed. "Ah, how little wives know of the trials that afflict husbands. Relations between me and Wolf are altogether at an end and I'm afraid there's nothing I can do about it."

"But, my dear husband, why worry about a fool like Wolf? You've always managed to win him over in the past. Surely you're not growing soft in your old age?"

Jackal took some comfort from his wife's words and went about his business as usual the next day, but he kept a wary eye open for Wolf nonetheless. He caught one of the farmer's sheep on a mountain crag and was busy cooking the meat over a fire.

The irresistible smell of the roasting meat drifted down to Wolf who was passing in the valley below. He looked up and

saw Jackal. "Say, Brother Jackal, won't you throw me a bit of that delicious meat? The cliff's too steep for me to climb," he said as if no hard feelings existed between them at all.

"Certainly, Brother Wolf!" replied Jackal. "Wait a moment while I cut off a nice big piece."

Wolf sat down beneath the crag and waited patiently. Jackal picked up a rounded rock that would fit in Wolf's mouth and tossed it into the fire. When it was red hot, he wrapped it in a piece of the sheep's caul and said: "The meat's perfectly cooked now, Brother Wolf. If you sit in exactly the right spot, I will drop it straight into your mouth."

Wolf duly positioned himself in what he thought was a direct line below Jackal and opened his jaws as wide as he could. "You're not quite close enough," said Jackal. "Move a little closer, will you?" Wolf moved closer. "A tad to the left," directed Jackal. Wolf moved to the left. "A little backwards," said Jackal. Wolf shifted backwards. "Now a little to the right," said Jackal. Wolf moved to the right.

Jackal took aim and dropped the hot rock straight down Wolf's throat. Wolf curled up in a convulsing ball. A very long time passed before he was able to get up and stagger home.

Golden pins, my story begins;
Golden fiddle, we've reached the middle;
Golden friends, my story ends!